a movie...and a book

a movie...
and a book

A NOVEL

DANIEL WAGNER

Alfred A. Knopf
New York
2004

Library of Congress Cataloging-in-Publication Data
Wagner, Daniel, [date].
A movie—and a book / by Daniel Wagner.
p. cm.
ISBN: 1-4000-4188-0
1. Islands—Fiction.   2. Castaways—Fiction.   3. Authorship—
Fiction.   I. Title.
PS3623.A356M68 2004
813'.6—dc22   2004002584

Manufactured in the United States of America
First Edition

To Trent and Billy,
my two favorite teachers

Acknowledgments

This book found its way to the wide open with the help of Tom Schmidlin, Alexis Lasheras, Fritz Bergstrom, Barbara J. Zitwer, Todd Siegal, Marty Asher, and Jennifer Jackson. Thank you so much.

a movie . . . and a book

the movie

We see a big empty room.

Of course, it's not a room the way we know them, with length, width, height, and all. It's just a room projected on a screen.

In a way, it's a dirty trick. We aren't used to empty rooms. Yet an empty room is understood in one glimpse. So after the short time it takes your brain to realize, *It's an empty room,* you start to wonder, *What for? Is it possible that the whole thing blows up all of a sudden? Or is it a lousy movie and they simply couldn't afford more?* And while thinking about it, while thinking about these kinds of things, the movie makers have you already glued to your seat. I guess they teach this stuff in art school nowadays.

As expected, the big empty room is still on the

screen ... and some whispering is already spreading through the theater—*What a setup.*

In a way, you can't blame the movie makers, though. It's us. It's our messed-up attention span. If you just start telling a nice story, right from the beginning no one is interested. Me neither, naturally. Sometimes I sit in front of the TV thinking about—

Hold on, an old guy enters the picture, holding a chair in his hands. He places the chair in the middle of the room and takes a seat. Basically he looks like a typical old man. He wears a baseball cap and old-fashioned glasses, and there is some excess skin around his mouth.

That's another trick. Just use a guy who looks a little funny—with too much skin around his mouth, for example—and the viewer, again, starts to think about it. Probably only half consciously you start to wonder if he had this excess skin even as a child. Then you try to picture him as a child. It doesn't make much sense, so your brain starts to look for other solutions. *It could be a side effect of arguing with his wife,* some might speculate. Others may even start to worry a little and wonder if gravity can do this over time.

That's how the brain works—and don't think the movie makers don't know it! They use your curiosity, they make you wonder, that's all they do; and while you're thinking about those things, you already start to relate to the characters. That's the whole trick.

I didn't even notice it. He's holding a book in his

hands. He gives it a little shake. He gives it another little shake . . . and the excess skin around his mouth joins the shake a little.

Now he's leafing through the book.

It looks as if he's starting to read from the book.

But no, he just looks up again, starting to speak. "They asked me to read this book to you. Actually, it's not a book; it's a movie they said." The way he's acting, it's clear he doesn't have any idea what's going on—they probably just picked him from the street and shoved some money in his pocket. All you need to do is take an old guy who doesn't have all his marbles, then give him an assignment—but make sure you don't explain it so well to him that he will behave awkwardly—and in nine out of ten cases it comes off as funny. No one knows why. But it's funny anyway.

He's leafing through the book again, as if he's not sure how to begin.

"I probably should start to read now."

Now he's looking all around the place for some sign of confirmation . . . a nodding head, or a thumbs-up from the movie director, I guess.

Someone probably nodded. In any case, the old guy puts his shaking index finger to the book, squints a little, and then finally starts to read.

"We see the outside of a suburban house from a moving perspective," he reads, then stops and sends a puzzled frown into the book again.

Ha! You should see what happens now. He twitches, as if a fly were bothering him on his neck.

"Ahhh . . . I guess that's a comment for the movie director," the old guy says.

Now he smiles proudly into the camera and the flesh around his mouth tightens a little.

"Okay, let's start again," he says, and clears his throat. "We see the outside of a suburban house from a moving perspective."

And now we see a suburban house on the screen.

Now we see the old guy again.

Now the suburb—

Now the ol—

I guess it's supposed to transition us into the movie. As if your brain slowly starts to picture the old guy's words.

We now see the suburban house continuously.

"The usual credits start to roll," the old guy reads.

Even though we now see this suburban house, we still hear the voice of the elderly guy. It's like you're looking at a picture book with your grandfather.

"The scene changes. We are now in the house, in a room that has been emptied for renovation," he reads.

And—*swoop*—there we see this room on the screen. Someone is painting something next to a window.

the shooting script

NARRATOR (*an elderly man*). Jim, a man in his forties, was holding a brush and a bucket of paint. He was drawing a decorative line on the wall next to the window. He stepped back to scrutinize his work—probably more to plan the next step than to dwell on his success so far. He looked irritated about something—the way a man must look when his wife has repeatedly told him to renovate some room he doesn't even like to use or something.

Jim was trying to give the window an ornamental frame. Again, he didn't look too happy.

Jim came to a decision.

(*We clearly see that he has come to a decision . . .*)

NARRATOR. He took a chair, and put it in front of the window. Then he stood on it and started to look for the beginning of the adhesive tape. First with his fingernails, then with his teeth. Finally he put the end of the tape on the wall. This time *over* the window—the same way he must have done earlier on the sides. It looked awkward. The chair was too small and he had to work so far over his head that he could hardly see what he was doing.

At this moment the door opened and Beth came in. She was eating an apple.

BETH. How's work progressing?

NARRATOR. Jim apparently couldn't hear her. Or he was so deep into the taping that he wasn't able—or in the mood—to process an answer. Right at this moment he ran out of tape.

JIM. Damn it.

BETH. What's wrong?

JIM. Tape's empty. Do you really think it needs a line over the window? I think it looks pretty good like this.

NARRATOR. It is obvious to the viewer that it needs one.

BETH, *still eating her apple.* No. It definitely needs one.

JIM, *exhausted.* So give me some tape.

(*We see a close-up on Beth's mouth chewing the apple.*)

NARRATOR. Jim was looking at Beth, annoyed at the way she ate her apple.

BETH. Hmm. (*She gives it another glance.*) If you lead your brush real carefully, you can do it without the tape.

JIM. Come on—I can hardly see it from down here. (*He sighs.*) I told you, we need a ladder.

BETH. You move the brush, and I'm going to lead you from back here. I can see it beautifully from here . . . Just move the brush real slow.

NARRATOR. Jim didn't care about the line anymore, so he put his brush to the left starting point.

BETH. Okay, you can start.

NARRATOR. Jim started to move the brush.

(*We see a close-up of the brush going over the wall.*)

BETH'S VOICE, *from behind.* A little up.

(*We keep looking at the moving brush.*)

BETH'S VOICE, *again.* Now down.

(*Our view cuts from the brush to Beth.*)

BETH. Up. (*She tries to focus better on the brush.*) I said up—you're still going down!

NARRATOR. Jim made a face toward the window.

BETH. Down. (*She observes it, then gets a little irritated.*) Down!

NARRATOR. This last comment from behind triggered something Jim couldn't—and didn't want to—control. He made a small but clearly exaggerated downward move.

BETH. Up! Up! Up!

NARRATOR. The already much-strained rubber band in Jim's mind snapped.

JIM, *stupidly mimicking Beth.* Up! Down! Up! Down! (*He looks back to Beth.*) What about this! (*He starts to move the brush up and down over the wall.*) Eh? What about that! Up! (*Up goes the brush.*) Down! (*Down goes the brush.*) Up! (*Up goes the brush.*) Down!

NARRATOR, *casually.* Another rubber band snapped.

BETH, *shouting.* Are you crazy? Are you absolutely crazy!?

NARRATOR. Jim started to echo again.

JIM. Are you *crazy?* (*And up goes the brush.*) Are you *abso*lutely *crazy?!* (*And down goes the brush, spreading paint all over the wall.*)

NARRATOR. A door slammed shut. Beth was gone. About two seconds later, the door opened with a jolt and Beth was striding in with shoe polish in her hand. She started to smear the shoe polish all over the other wall.

BETH, *shouting.* What about that . . . eh? What about that!

At this moment the scene cuts with a black flash and we are hovering over the ocean. The elastic surface reflects gray-green patterns, the way it does on cloudy summer days. The song "Blanket" by Imogen Heap with Urban Species starts to play. It gives the cloudy weather something snug. The credits continue to roll.

We keep looking at the surface of the water. After a while some single raindrops start to hit. Then the rain gets a little heavier.

The camera starts to move now, floating over the water. Gradually the rain ceases.

After a moment—a moment long enough to make us forget the first scene, and long enough for us to get caught up in the peacefulness of the music and the ocean—the camera starts to level up and we can see the horizon. In front of us is a small island. We are heading toward it.

We float for some time along the sandy shoreline, with the cloudy horizon to the left. Then we spot two people on the shore. We float a little closer to them.

part one

1.

"I don't know," said Lou, lying on his back in the sand. "And in a way, I don't even care."

Liz was looking toward the ocean. She was sitting right next to Lou in the sand. It was a special sitting position she had, with her arms closely around her pulled-in legs—the way someone sits to keep warm on a cloudy summer day on the beach. It's especially recommended if you're wearing only a dark blue bikini, along with a comfortable gray sweater with a hood. The way she looked at the ocean was the way a small girl would, safely at her mother's side after she had just seen a young bird lying dead on the curbstone. She had glassy eyes and there was something dreamy about them.

"It looks like rain again," she said.

"I don't care," came from the body to her right. "Rain is beauty."

"You're crazy," she said, and shivered a little, pulling her naked legs a little closer.

"I'm not."

"You definitely are."

"I'm not," Lou said. "I'm just a misunderstood Chinese intellectual."

"You're not," Liz said, pulling her shoulders up a little. It brought the hood of her sweater a little closer around her neck. "You're American."

Lou kept looking toward the sky for a moment. Then he said, "What are you?"

"What do you mean?"

"How would you describe yourself if you had to?"

"I'm me."

"You're boring," said Lou, and shook his head methodically from side to side, shaping the mold in the sand a little deeper. "Try it—try to tag a label on yourself. It isn't that easy," he challenged. Then he added, "You know, just for fun."

Liz didn't answer. She was looking toward the sea.

Lou raised his head a little to see what she was doing.

The wind blew a strand of hair over her face. She brushed it away.

Lou observed it with interest, kept his head suspended for a moment, then lowered it back to the sand.

"I'm the only normal person in the world," she finally said.

"*Ha!* That's great!" Lou smiled toward the clouds. "That's certainly a be—"

He started.

Distant thunder had interrupted his pleasure. He sat up to look at the big black cloud over the ocean. After a moment he lowered himself back into the sand. "Did you know that I kind of like it here?"

Liz seemed to be listening but didn't say anything.

"I like it here because we have an assignment," he said. "It wouldn't be the same if we had planned to get here. If we had planned it, it would be totally different."

Liz still didn't say anything, but just lowered her chin to rest on her kneecaps. It seemed to be a better position to look dreamily at the ocean.

"It's a game . . . It's a movie and it's a book," Lou continued, then thought it over. "Do you know what a movie and book are?"

"What do you mean? Of course I know it," said Liz. "A book is written on p—"

"I don't mean that," Lou interrupted. "It's a saying."

He closed his eyes.

"Or, better, it's something like a philosophy of life."

With the word *philosophy* he raised his eyebrows a little.

He pressed his lips together.

"The philosophy of the *Japanese intellectuals*, I guess."

"Ha, you're so funny," said Liz. "First you are this great, but misunderstood, *Chinese intellectual*, and now you are a Japanese intellectual."

She was smiling at Lou while rolling her eyes.

"Okay, okay." Lou was amused. "Let's make it a great, misunderstood *Eastern* intellectual then, if you will."

For a moment neither of them said anything. And only the sound of the small waves and the light wind coming in from the sea kept the place from indulging in a complete silence.

"So what's behind the saying? What did you call it again . . . a movie and a book?" said Liz after a while. "So what's the big wisdom of the saying . . . if there is any?"

"Oh, there's a lot of wisdom," Lou asserted, wagging his head seriously in the sand. "If you know what a movie and a book are, if you really know what it means, you start to—I don't know, I guess you just start to look at life a little differently."

"So, a movie and a book?" said Liz. "I never heard of it."

"Maybe it's just a family saying. I don't know," said Lou. "My father used to say it. I was never sure he got the wisdom of it, though—I guess he just picked it up from his brother."

A moment of silence followed.

"So what does it mean?"

"In a way, it just helps you to get over two difficult situations in life, that's all," said Lou. Then after a moment he said, "A movie is the first situation, it's when something strange or crazy happens to you. It could be something as stupid as walking into a pole, for example."

Lou looked for a moment toward the clouds in silence, then he blinked a couple of times.

"The interesting thing is, if stuff like this happens to *someone else*, it's highly funny and entertaining. But if it happens to you, it all of a sudden doesn't seem that funny anymore. It's rather trying."

Lou stopped again, and by rolling his head to the right he looked at Liz.

She was looking out at the ocean.

Lou evened his head back into a more natural position and reflected for a moment. "But it's not trying for the person who understands the saying. Of course, it hurts them just as much as anyone else if they walk into a stupid pole," said Lou, "but they don't forget—in the heat of the moment—that life is a movie and that for the audience this situation is highly entertaining . . . So they just step a little out of themselves and share the amusement with the audience. That's all they do—that's the whole secret behind it!"

Lou kept looking to the sky for a moment. Then he raised his head a little and said, "Do you know what I mean?"

"Kind of," said Liz.

All of a sudden Lou's stare lit up. "So, say my father,

for example, secretly had planned the whole thing, staged the whole crazy thing to bring us together. It would be a movie," he said dryly but with amusement in his voice.

Liz looked to Lou, rolling her eyes. There was amusement in her look too, however guarded.

Lou saw it from the corner of his eye and enjoyed having successfully confirmed his "craziness." He added seriously, "Observe your life from the third person, and if it's funny or strange, it's a movie."

"And what's the use of this *wisdom,* if I may ask?"

"What's the use? Hell, it's pretty clear. Put two people in the same situation, and the normal guy gets angry, while the guy with *wisdom* is amused."

"It's escaping into a dream-world. It's not facing reality," said Liz. She seemed to be a little worried again.

Lou didn't say anything.

"What's a book, then?" said Liz after a while.

"A book," Lou said after a short moment of suspense, "is when something dramatic is happening to you. It could be something sad, a difficult situation, or lovesickness, for example. Or just a rainy day." He thought it over, his focus still on the clouds. "Everyone knows the books. *Oliver Twist, The Catcher*—or even *Heidi,* for God's sake. Someone tries to find a way through something difficult, or something sad—that's basically all." Lou stopped for a beat. "The interesting thing is, for the person *in* the book, it may sometimes be a little difficult, or sad. But you, reading the story, you feel kind of cozy about it. You feel a little sad too, like the person in the book, but at the same time something beautiful happens in your heart. I guess you've read these stories too?"

Liz nodded, looking toward the sea.

"So, if we secretly were falling in love on this island, and then we died—right in the rain—before even having an affair, it would be a book," Lou said. "It would be a story full of desire, full of courage—and, of course, full of melancholy."

Liz rolled her eyes again.

Another clap of thunder came from the sea.

"But what's the wisdom? What do you get from it?" Liz said, looking at Lou.

"Well," he said, "a person with the wisdom in a situation like this feels a little cozy too. Right when feeling sad. He's able to see what the third person—reading the book, so to speak—can see."

Liz thought for a moment, still looking toward the sea.

The wind was stronger now; it carried the black clouds a little closer to the island.

"Don't you think we might die here?" said Liz reflectively.

"I don't know. All I know is before I die I will have fought it as best I can."

Liz didn't say anything for a while. Then all of a sudden her face lit up a little, as if she had thought of something clever. "I guess you feel a little sad, but cozy, right now?" she said with a trace of a new spirit in her voice.

"No," he deadpanned, "I just like sitting here and talking with you."

Liz smiled a little. Then shivered.

"Sometimes you're nice," she said. She said it loud enough to be heard but not loud enough to be a part of the conversation.

But Lou couldn't accept it just like that. "That's obvious. Everyone likes a Chinese intellectual."

"Sometimes you're a moron too," she said, and this new spirit completely took over.

Slowly, but gradually, the clouds that had hung over the ocean began to break and rain started to fall.

Both stood up.

"You know what?" said Liz, "I don't mind the rain."

"You're crazy," Lou teased.

"No, I'm an *intellectual Chinese*."

With the word *Chinese*, she turned and ran ahead. Lou didn't follow—he just watched her run. The way she was moving reminded him of a child running in her favorite but really oversize sweater.

2.

We are in a kitchen. If we take a good look we see that it's the kitchen of the suburban house we saw in the intro. There's Beth, whom we already got to know, working behind the sink. And on the tiled floor lies a young boy. He could be ten, maybe eleven.

"Pete, don't bother the cat while she's eating."

"I'm not bothering her," said Pete, lying on his stomach next to the cat, his chin resting on his flat palms. "I'm just observing her."

"I don't want you lying on the cold floor."

"Mother?" said Pete, showing no intention of removing himself from the allegedly cold floor. "Do we still have that small box with the holes in the lid—I mean the one we used to put the bait in?"

"I don't know. It could be in the garage. Why? What do you need it for?"

"I don't need it. I just wondered," said Pete. He slid his right hand from under his chin and reached for the cat. For a moment he tried to hold the cat's hind leg to the floor with two fingers.

"Pete. I don't like what I heard from Sarah this morning," said Beth, looking down at Pete. "She said you threatened to put a spider on her bed. And you know how she feels about spiders."

"I was just kidding," said Pete.

One part of the cat continued to eat, and another part tried to pull its leg out of the hold.

"But it isn't nice, anyway. You know how she's afraid of spiders."

"I only said I discovered a small spider in my room behind a seashell," said Pete in his defense, looking up at his mother for the first time. "Well, I just asked her if she hates small spiders too."

He must have let go of the hold while changing his focal point, so the cat, still eating, pulled its leg away.

"That's not what she told me," said Beth, cleaning another leaf of lettuce. "She told me you showed her the spider."

"Yes, I showed it to her. But she said it was too small to really scare her," said Pete, looking back at the cat.

The cat had its head suspended over the bowl now, concentrating on chewing a big chunk.

"Didn't you say you planned to feed it with flies to make it a big one? Sarah said you threatened to put it on her bed one day, when it's big enough."

"I was just kidding," said Pete. "I said one day I'm going to put the spider *underneath a cup* on her bed. But when I do it, I'll just put an empty cup on her bed."

"That's not nice. That's really not nice, Pete. You

know she won't go near the cup, and in the end it's me who has to—"

She stopped as she saw Pete pursuing the cat out of the kitchen. He walked four-legged and in slow motion, pretending to be some hideous beast of nature.

3.

We are back on the island. It's night.

"Are you asleep?" Liz asked.

"No."

"I can't sleep." She turned and tried to make a picture out of the darkness. But she saw only that Lou was lying supine, looking to the sky. She moved into the same position, then said, "Are you afraid of the dark?"

"No."

"Do you like the stars?"

"Yes."

"Are you afraid of dying?"

"No."

"Do you like the sea?"

"Yes."

"Do you believe in something after— Oh . . . did you see that shooting star?"

"There wasn't one."

"You have to make a wish," said Liz.

"There wasn't even a shooting star."

Liz wasn't listening. After a moment she said, "Did you make a wish?"

"Yes."

"What did you wish?"

"I could tell you, but then I'd have to shoot you," Lou said casually.

"Oh, come on. What was it?"

"If you tell, it won't come true," he said and added, "That's the rule."

Liz just said, "Oh."

After a moment she said, "I can't sleep. Tell me a good-night story."

"No. You tell me one."

"No," she wailed. "Please tell me one."

"All right. But let me think first."

4.

In Pete's bedroom. The same night.

Pete was lying in his bed saying his prayer: "Dear God, please make Mom and Dad a little more cool." He thought for a moment, then went on, "Besides, I'm looking forward to tomorrow's class trip. I hope that the weather's going to be nice."

5.

Back on the island. A moment later.

"And?" said Liz.

"I told you I have to think first."

"But not that long."

"As long as it takes to make up a story."

"Why don't you tell me one you already know? Don't you know a story from your childhood or anything?"

"Yes," said Lou, "but I don't feel like telling a children's story right now."

"So tell me your favorite story out of all the stories you've ever read."

He thought for a moment. "There is one I really like a lot. It's about this guy named Tim," he said. "I guess Tim isn't even his real name, because he lives somewhere in China—they probably just translated it that way, the poor bastards."

Lou thought about it for a moment.

"But I can't tell it—it's way too long. You would be asleep before I even came to anything."

"So tell me your favorite part of it."

Lou thought for a moment. "There is this part that's really great." He stopped and seemed to reconsider it, but then started anyway. "This guy, Tim, lived somewhere in a city, but he used to spend two days a week on a farm. It was actually his uncle's farm. But his uncle didn't live there anymore. He had given up farming and moved to the city too. But he kept the house for the weekends, or something. Anyway, Tim went there to write his stories, and he had a piano there that he always played till late at night. It was totally out in the country. As a matter of fact, he had to ride his bicycle for about two hours to get there. But it wasn't a big deal for him . . . you know, these Asian guys love to ride their bicycles. The great part is, there was this other farm near this house, and the dog of this farm always came to Tim on the days he stayed there. It's impossible to explain—you have to read it."

"Come on," pleaded Liz.

"All right. But don't complain if you don't like it," said Lou.

He was thinking for a moment.

"So the dog likes Tim a lot, and Tim likes the dog a lot," he said, making an effort to sound bored.

Liz started to laugh.

"Why are you laughing?"

"You know why," said Liz, amused.

Lou's face lit up a little. Then he tried to concentrate.

"All right, let's have a little quiet in here, or no story," Lou said, remembering a line of some other book.

There came no response. Liz probably hadn't read this book, so it may have seemed a little weird to her.

"If Tim, for example, played the piano in his room, the dog always lay outdoors and listened. He usually played the piano till late at night. And before he went to sleep he would go out and say good night to the dog.

"So one night—it was a really clear night with the sky full of stars—he went out to say good night to the dog. He sat down next to it and stroked it. When the dog got special attention, he would always stretch full length with this benign expression on his face," Lou explained, and thought for a moment. "You know, the way dogs do." He stopped for another beat, fully aware that his listener, next to him, was waiting for more information. After a pause he continued.

"Anyway, one particular night both sat there in front of the house watching the stars." Lou stopped again, thinking for a moment. "The great thing is, Tim always enjoyed breathing the warm evening air while sitting there with his dog. You know how the air is when a long winter comes to an end and the first spring day arrives, and the air is all of a sudden warm and fresh as hell, like in the evening?"

"Yes," Liz said.

"When you read the book, you almost feel as if you could capture a short breath of this air yourself. Anyway, where did I stop?"

"You said Tim was sitting one *particularly fresh* night with the dog, watching the stars."

"Ah, yes," he said, with a sparkle in his eye. "And then Tim said to the dog, 'This was another glorious day, wasn't it? But dogs don't care about stuff like that, do they?' And the dog only sprawled a little more, enjoying the attention. Then Tim poked the dog's soft belly with his finger, to get his attention, I guess, or just to tease him. And then comes the best part—the part I like most. The dog lifted his head up to see what was going on, still with that benign, stupid expression. Tim, seeing it, was filled with affection, groped the dog's neck with both hands, and shook the fur, saying, 'Soon you're going to get tired. Then you'll fall asleep and the world will make another turn. And in the morning, when the sun comes up on the other side, you'll wake up and another day will begin. And right now you don't have the slightest idea.' "

Lou thought about it for a moment. Then: "Isn't that the most beautiful story? It's especially great if you read it. It's really one of the best books."

There came no response. Liz either was thinking or had fallen asleep. It was the first, though, and she said, "Well, it's not the best story I've ever heard, but it's kind of cute."

"Most people don't like stories like this. They think stuff has to explode all the time, or people have to run around naked and all. Or things have to be cute as hell," said Lou. "I don't even think it's cute. I know what you mean, though. In a way, if you read it, it's cute. But you never get the feeling this guy wrote it down because he wanted it to be cute. Neither do you get the feeling he wrote it down because he wanted it to come off as smart.

It's hard to find a book like this. It's really great. You really should read it."

"What's it all about? What's the story?"

"There isn't really a story. It's just personal stuff from this Chinese guy's life. Stuff he observes. Stuff he likes. Stuff he doesn't like. Stuff that makes him excited. Stuff that worries him. That's basically all."

6.

The next day: It's early morning. We are at a subway station. There is Jim (the man with the brush and bucket from the intro) and Arnold. Arnold is African-American. He's about fourteen.

"Mr. Frazier," said Arnold, "I ran into my uncle yesterday. He has this friend who's an agent. I thought—maybe I could ask him to read your script if you want me to."

"That's mighty nice. Thank you, Arnold, but I'll have to find my own way," Jim said with a certain awkwardness.

"I read there were hundreds of great writers that couldn't publish their work for years and years and then they became really big."

"Really?" said Jim.

"Wouldn't it be great if you hit it big time? Would you still keep working?"

"Probably not, Arnold."

"That really would be something, Mr. Frazier, you becoming a famous writer," said Arnold, thinking it over with a big smile on his face.

7.

On the island.

The sun slowly rose behind the ocean, reflecting on the water through a light mist.

Lou was running to the shore. He dove into a wave, then started to swim.

Liz was waking up. She stretched her arms and legs, shivered a little, then looked sleepily to the sea.

Lou shouted, "Come into the water! It's so refreshing."

Liz shivered again, then tried to wrap her sweater a little tighter around her body, still looking sleepily to the sea.

8.

We are in a supermarket.

Arnold was working behind a cash register, being friendly with the customers. Next to him in another register booth worked Jim, not so enthusiastically. An old lady was packing her stuff into the bag behind Jim's booth.

Jim turned and said, "Do you want the receipt?" holding it in her direction.

The old lady looked at him, and said, "No," with a seductive smile, as if she were doing Jim a big favor. Then she added casually, while passing her hand dismissively through the air, "I don't need it," as if she considered herself not only cool as hell, but pretty worldly too.

Jim crumbled the receipt and threw it with a frown into the garbage can next to his feet.

Arnold must have caught a glimpse of Jim's face. "Do you know her, Mr. Frazier?"

Jim looked at him. "No . . . no, Arnold. But call me Jim, I told you before."

"I know, I just feel more comfortable calling you Mr. Frazier," said Arnold, with a big smile.

9.

On the island. Noon.

The hut they were building was right next to a small river coming out of the woods. They had built a fire. Lou was sitting on a piece of log eating a fish on a wooden stick. Liz squatted next to the fire, still holding hers over the heat.

"Do you think it was fate that brought us here?" she said, looking at Lou behind her. She focused back on her fish. "In a way, it's pretty beautiful."

"I don't know," said Lou, taking a bite of his fish. "We are here, that's all we need to know."

"I know, but do you think there's a plan behind it?"

"There's a plan behind everything in nature."

Liz kept holding the stick over the fire for a while in silence. She moved it in small circles, then turned it. "But do you think there is a bad and dark side of nature too? You know—do you believe in a bad and dark side, or anything?"

Taking almost the last bite, Lou said, "The dark side is when we take stuff as a personal offense instead of trying to find a way. This kind of stuff doesn't look good to the third person. It looks horrible."

Liz was inspecting her fish closely, smelling it. "I'm

going to try this now," she said, and stepped back to the second log.

Lou took the last bite, then threw the fish bones over his shoulder into the woods.

10.

In the subway. Evening.

Arnold sat in a subway car, flirting with a baby in a buggy.

Not too far away Jim sat in another seat. No doubt, Arnold would have chosen the seat next to Jim if he had had the choice. But during certain hours subway cars have their own rules. Sometimes you can sit next to each other. Sometimes you can't. Jim seemed thankful for the break. Yet he didn't look completely happy. About three yards in front of him a homeless guy was playing the flute.

The subway car slowed down, then stopped.

The guy with the flute used this quiet spell for a part that required him to play with restricted pressure, while at the same time—it was obvious—compensating for the subdued volume with emotion. Jim listened a moment, then got distracted by a scene that took place on the platform about twenty feet away from his window.

A construction worker had started to operate a pneumatic hammer. But the noise drowned out the sound of the flute only for a moment, then stopped. Jim observed the construction worker trying to lever a curbstone with his machine.

The stone apparently wasn't doing what it should.

The construction worker was frustrated and started to jerk his hammer around. Up and down. Side to side.

It still wouldn't work.

Jim checked back on the guy with the flute. He was at an especially emotional part, moving his head from side to side and beating time softly with his left foot. Jim smiled, then snorted, then shook his head slightly. He looked back out the window. His ears kept focusing on the soft sound of the flute while his eyes were on the construction worker, still jerking up and down with his blunt machine.

The car started to move. The pneumatic hammer started up again.

The noise of the hammer swallowed the flute for a moment, then faded as the car moved on.

Jim looked around to check if anyone else had witnessed the tableau. But everyone seemed to be absorbed in something else, or nothing at all. With a cynical smile, Jim shook his head again and thought for a moment, then looked back to Arnold.

He saw Arnold happily interacting with the baby's mother.

11.

On the island. Evening.

The sun was lingering over the orange horizon of the sea. Lou and Liz were lying by the shore. Lou lay on his stomach, his chin supported on his right fist. Liz, again, sat with her arms around her drawn-in legs. They didn't speak for a long time.

After a while Lou looked at Liz, probably to see what she was doing or where she was looking.

She was looking out to sea.

He looked back to the sea himself, readjusting his chin on his fist.

A moment later he looked at Liz again. "Do you think it's boring just sitting here, not talking at all?" said Lou.

"No."

A beat of silence followed. Lou lowered his chin back to his fist.

The silence held on for a moment.

"You know, people usually think they are having fun only while they're talking, making lots of jokes," said Lou. "I mean, they think you're kind of a bore if you aren't entertaining other people all the time."

"I know."

The sun was a half circle now and almost dark red.

The only sound came from the small waves that periodically slid to the shore.

"Lou?"

"Huh?"

"Isn't it beautiful here? The air, do you smell it?" asked Liz.

"I certainly do."

It was quiet.

"Lou?"

"Huh?"

"I just had a thought," said Liz.

"What thought?"

"What if the world is a being? . . . Maybe something more like a plant, though. And what if it needs us for some reason?" she said. "It's possible."

Lou kept watching the remaining bit of sun.

". . . it needs us for some reason like we need bacteria for some reason."

The sun was down now. The only thing that proved that it had ever existed was a remaining brighter field of light. Liz felt extremely comfortable, and Lou said thank you to the writer.

12.

The Fraziers' home. Evening.

Pete sat on the sofa, watching TV. Next to him sat Sarah. She was around six. She had blond hair that was long but didn't quite reach her shoulders. It was cut in a straight line just a little above her shoulders—that's the way it was. They were watching a cartoon.

Pete wasn't really watching, though. He was looking all around the room, looking for trouble. Then back at the TV. Then at his watch.

Now he was looking at Sarah.

She sat there with her mouth slightly open, enjoying the cartoon.

Pete kept looking at her for a while. Then said, *"Hey."*

Sarah turned her head slowly, looking at Pete like a lady would—like a bored lady, though. She knew what might be in store. *"Hey, what?"*

"Close your mouth when you're watching TV," said Pete, starting to grin.

Sarah just made a face at him, then started to focus on the cartoon again. Finally she said, "Close your own mouth when you're watching TV."

This time it was Pete who gave a grimace, but Sarah didn't see it.

Jim came in. "Hi, guys."

Pete was all too glad to strike up a conversation. "Hi, Dad. How was work?"

"Not too bad. You know, it's only temporary."

"You've been saying that for a very long time," said Pete.

Sarah gave an annoyed look toward the two conversationalists. But neither of them took notice.

"How was your day, was it all right? Your field trip?" asked Jim.

"It was all right."

Sarah switched off the TV, jumped down from the sofa, and left the room.

"Just *all right*? That doesn't sound like much. What happened?"

"Nothing, just this new guy . . . that came from *California*. He gets on your nerves sometimes."

"You know how life is," said Jim. "Life is a game: it's a movie and it's a book. It's not always easy, but there is always a way. You just have to look at it the right way."

"I know, I know . . . I'm just a little tired of him being the big shot all the time."

"I guess he got Jane's attention?"

"*Dad.*"

Jim made two steps to the window. Looking out into the darkness, he said, "Is Mom around?"

"She won't come home till late. She called from her office. By the way, Uncle Andy called."

"Oh," said Jim, his curious expression reflected in the window.

13.

Night. Island.

"What about building comfortable beds in the hut?" Liz said, lying next to Lou in the darkness.

"Excellent idea."

"I always feel exhausted in the morning from sleeping on these palm fronds."

Lou didn't respond. He just said, "Tell me a good-night story. It's your turn."

"What kind of a story?"

"I don't know . . . the story of the girl that always felt exhausted in the morning from sleeping on palm fronds."

"You're so funny."

Lou was enjoying her reaction. He lay on his back—the usual way—and looked at the stars.

"I know a story."

"So tell it," said Lou.

"But it's scary."

"I'm ready."

"But I'm not sure if I am. Will you comfort me if I get scared?"

"I might, and I might not," said Lou.

"What do you mean?" asked Liz.

"Nothing. But we can hold hands if you get scared," Lou said casually.

"You're pretty aloof sometimes. Why is that? Do you dislike me?"

"I'm not aloof. I'm just not the guy that hugs everyone on first sight, that's all."

"What kind of guy are you, then?"

"I don't know. I like people physically at the same distance that I have them mentally, I guess. I don't see the point in being all close to someone physically while only making small talk."

"I'm sorry that I appear to be a small-talk person to you."

"It has nothing to do with you."

Liz started to smile, then started to say something, then thought better of it. Her smile faded for a moment while she seemed to concentrate on a thought.

After a moment she said, "All right," and her face lit up again. "Let me tell you a good-night story. Take it as an act of charity to your cold and lonesome heart."

A spell of silence followed.

"What about the story?" Lou asked.

Liz began as if Lou hadn't said anything. "It's the story of the guy with the cold heart," she said, hiding her pride in the darkness.

"Ha, ha. You're so funny."

She dismissed his comment and continued: "It all started somewhere in a small village where the guy with the cold heart grew up. When he was a little boy, his parents used to go hiking with their friends. These friends had a daughter, and she was the only normal person in the world.

"The only normal person in the world was very stubborn and she didn't like hiking at all, but she was very fond of the older guy with the cold heart. So when he was there too, she walked over every imaginable mountain, partially to be near him and partially to impress him. But it was in vain—you couldn't impress the guy with the cold heart so easily.

"Over the years they grew apart. They saw each other in the village sometimes, but the guy with the cold heart wasn't very friendly. After about ten years he didn't even recognize her anymore . . . too cold was his heart," she pointed out, trying to observe Lou. But she didn't see his smile.

She continued, "Then something happened—something very atypical for the guy with the cold heart. He met her again by accident and they started to speak. They talked about their childhood, and time passed very quickly. They realized that both were interested in sailing, and the unbelievable happened: the guy with the cold heart invited her for a day on his father's boat. To this day no one knows why he invited her, but rumor has it that he did it because he secretly liked her, though he has denied that vehemently." Once again she tried to read his expression, but it was too dark out.

She thought for a moment, then was about to continue but stopped before the first word was out. She thought a little longer, then said, "They met a couple of times to sail. Then something mysterious happened." All of a sudden her playful mood changed and some fear crept into her voice. "They were out at sea. It was a normal day, not dangerously stormy or anything . . . And the next thing they knew they were stranded with a torn rubber boat on a small island."

Lou didn't say anything. He was thinking.

"It's pretty strange what happened, isn't it?"

"Yes."

"What could it have been? Do you think the sailboat started to burn and we somehow rescued ourselves in the small boat, only half conscious, and then fell in a coma from the smoke or something?"

"Possibly."

"Or do you think there is some magical force out there that transports people to different places? Or are we dead and this is just an illusion?"

"I don't know," said Lou.

"It's pretty scary."

"I don't think so. Something happened that made us leave the sailboat. That's all."

"Maybe the devil made us leave the boat to come to this place where he's going to torture us."

"Maybe," said Lou. "Maybe I'm the devil."

"Stop that."

"Maybe I'm just waiting for the right time to kill you."

"Stop it!"

Both jumped.

A distant clap of thunder rolled over the sea. It wasn't especialy loud, but it rumbled ominously through the darkness.

"I'm scared," Liz said.

Whrromp!

This one was pretty loud. Both froze. Liz moved close to Lou.

"It's just a thunderstorm," Lou reassured her, and added, "It'll pass over the ocean," hoping he was right.

A long silence followed. Both were trying to prepare for the next roll of thunder so as not to be startled. But nothing happened—all they saw was distant lightning that brightened the sea now and then.

"I have to pee," said Liz.

"So go."

"Never alone."

"What do you expect, me to stand guard?"

"Just come along a couple of yards."

"You don't have to go that far, and besides, it stopped anyway."

"All right. I'll go alone."

"But don't go too far," said Lou.

"*Ha.* I guess somebody is scared."

She got up and looked around. It was too dark to make anything out. A distant bolt of lightning helped her, but it also took away some of her newfound courage. She walked a few steps toward the beach, then looked back. It was too dark to see Lou. She took another couple of steps, almost testing her own bravery. She felt frightened and excited at the same time. She felt like testing her courage again and took another few steps.

14.

At the same time, right behind in the underbrush.

A mysterious figure was moving cautiously through the woods. It observed Liz with the help of a faraway lightning bolt, then made another stealthy step.

15.

Back to Liz and Lou.

"Where are you going?" Lou said through the darkness.

Liz didn't answer. She wanted him to get a little scared.

All of a sudden she heard some crackling noises coming out of the woods. She started, then listened.

Nothing.

She slipped her bikini down and squatted.

Lou had heard the crackling too. He was suspended on his elbow now, looking toward the underbrush.

Nothing.

Whrromp! Another clap of thunder bounced off the sea.

Both were paralyzed for a moment. After the shock wore off, Liz felt excited from the adrenaline. She ended her business, pulled up her bikini, and ran back to Lou.

"Damn, my bladder nearly ripped me apart," she said, excited.

"It's a bitch. Life in the wilderness," Lou said.

Both felt great, still buzzing from the thunder.

16.

Back in the underbrush.

The figure in the woods tried to find orientation. Then slowly it moved farther into the woods, bustled around by a tree for a moment, then beat it.

part two

17.

We hear the sound of a train traveling over its rails. Shrubby landscape is passing on the other side of the glass. It's about noon on a sunny summer day.

Jim was looking out the window.

After some time the train slowed down, then stopped.

Jim kept looking out the window.

The train started to move again, slowly gaining speed.

Jim probably saw her from the corner of his eye. Right next to him, in the aisle, stood a woman searching for a seat. He looked up at her.

With an open purse in her left hand, a monstrosity of a flower bouquet in her right hand, and the ticket between her lips, she signaled something in the direction of the empty seats.

"It's all yours," said Jim, looking up at her, then out the window again.

The woman started to rearrange her belongings busily.

Jim's position wasn't only perfect for observing the outdoors, but also great for sneaking a good look at the train's interior. Using the soft reflection in the glass, Jim stealthfully observed his neighbors.

In the reflection, two hands were putting the flowers on the seat opposite him. There was also a pair of nice legs. Jim took a look at them, enjoying his isolated vantage point.

The woman, on the other hand, took the ticket from between her lips, and while doing so she looked at Jim. She saw his fixed stare toward the glass. It looked funny, so she smiled a little.

Sometimes you don't see the full picture in the reflection.

Her face appeared on the glass as she sat down. She was still fiddling around in her purse.

At this moment, Jim's expression changed from that of a man secretly observing a beautiful woman to that of a man slightly puzzled.

He took another look at the reflection.

She was closing her purse.

After a brief period of hesitation, he looked up and said, "Now it dawns on me why everyone is running around with flowers. Today is Mother's Day, isn't it?"

"Yes, it is," said the woman with a sigh and a conversational frown.

Jim sighed and said, "Now I'm relieved. I knew it was Mother's Day—I just wanted to hear you speak. It may sound stupid, but I just asked so I could hear your voice. You look exactly like my brother's girlfriend, and I have only met her once, just for a minute. So I wanted to hear you speak to check and see if you're her or not."

The woman only looked at Jim, not saying a word.

"Don't get me wrong. I just thought I had to make sure you weren't his girlfriend. You know, it would have been pretty awkward if you had been her, and I would have been sitting here just looking out the window." Jim stopped, trying to find better words. "See, it would have been pretty funny if we both had just sat here looking out the window; and then gotten out at the same station—still not speaking at all—and then walked to the same house, just a couple of feet away. You know, without speaking a word or anything. And then, right at the door of my brother's apartment, we would have realized that we should have known each other, and that we at least should have said a few words. That would have been pretty embarrassing," Jim said, and laughed nervously, indicating that such a situation would be an awful spot for anyone.

The woman held her gaze, but there was some amusement in it now. Then she started to smile.

"I mean, it would have been pretty awkward, don't you think?" asked Jim nervously.

The woman thought about it for a moment. "That's about the funniest thing I've heard today," she said. "But why are you relieved I'm not your brother's girlfriend?"

"I'm just not that good at small talk, that's why. And here in the train, sitting right next to each other, you're almost forced to say something. It becomes pretty awkward. You know, sometimes it's hard if you're supposed to talk and you can't think of anything to talk about."

"It probably is. I've never thought about it that way," said the woman, still amused.

"Yes," said Jim, who apparently couldn't think of anything else to say about it.

The train kept moving on.

18.

On the island at about the same time.

Lou was climbing a rock, sweating. The sun shone on his tanned arms. It was a hot summer day, and there was little wind.

Liz already stood on top of the rock, looking down. "Come on, what's up?" she called down.

"Look, I want to enjoy the climb. If you go up all in a hurry, it's no fun."

Liz laughed, rolling her eyes. It seemed she was in high spirits from being better at something. "Let's meet at the top," she shouted down, and disappeared out of Lou's sight.

He climbed a little faster.

Liz hid in a cleft at the side of the small platform.

Lou looked down; his sight began to blur. He focused up again, gathered courage, and continued to climb. Finally he dragged himself over the edge. He looked around but couldn't spot Liz. Then, standing, he looked up.

He still couldn't see her.

All of a sudden he heard someone laughing—it came from the crevice, of course.

Lou looked around. He seemed a little insecure.

Liz jumped out from her hiding place with a big grin. "Pretty clumsy, you are," she said, and licked the corners of her lips. "But it's cute on you." Then she turned to look at the sea, or just in the general direction of the sea.

"Look, if you think you're such a superior climber, what about a little contest, then?"

"Whatever you want," Liz said, slowly turning, still beaming.

"So you take this face and I'll take the one on the other side. Whoever first reaches the top is the better climber."

"That's not fair. We have to climb the same route," she protested.

"I'm not going to climb if someone is staring at me and judging my style," he said, and added, "while feeling so *superior*."

"All right. But let's switch the routes."

"Whatever you want," Lou said, but it was clear he was trying to seem casual about it.

19.

On the train again.

For a short moment Jim wasn't sure if she had caught his eye in the reflection. He felt the urge to say something.

As if feeling the pressure of the situation too—or maybe she had really caught his eye in the reflection—the woman spoke up and said, "Are you visiting your mother too?"

"No, I'm going to visit my brother."

"Oh, yes, I guess I should have known," she said. "So your brother has a girlfriend that looks like me?"

"Very much so. Yes."

"Is she a nice person?"

"I guess she is, but I don't know her that well."

"Oh, yes. I guess I should have known that too," she said. "I guess she must be, if she's the girlfriend of your brother."

"I wouldn't be too sure about that," said Jim, animated.

The woman smiled.

"He's pretty unpredictable, my brother. Always full of energy, full of *great* ideas."

He had her full attention now.

"He's about forty. And do you know what he still does all the time?"

"No."

"He plays these crazy video games. The ones where you have a steering wheel on the table and an acceleration pedal under the table." Jim shook his head. "God, it looks so stupid if you come in and he's sitting in the middle of the living room behind the steering wheel, with the TV going full blast. He's way too old for that kind of stuff."

"Well, if he likes it. Why shouldn't he, if he likes it?"

"The crazy thing is, if you call him, and he's in the middle of some race, he doesn't even answer the phone. He says you destroy the whole spirit. He's quite a character," said Jim, shaking his head.

The woman smiled for a while, seeking Jim's eyes. But Jim was looking at the bunch of flowers. Then something snapped her back into her own world. Her expression changed instantly. "*Oh,* I have to hurry now. I'm sorry. Next stop is my stop," said the woman. She started to pack her stuff.

20.

Back on the island.

Liz already stood on top of the next small rock face, looking down. "Come on, what's up?" she called down again.

Lou didn't process a reply, probably not because he was in a bad mood but simply because he was out of breath. At least, he wasn't the kind of person that got irritated about such things. He was the kind of person who gave it his all—exhausted every idea to the limit, but when it was clear he'd lost, he'd lost.

After a moment he once again dragged himself over the edge and lay, exhausted, on his back, sweating and breathing wildly.

Liz looked at him, by now sitting on top of a stone. She didn't say anything; she just looked at him.

"You're cute," she said, observing Lou's reaction.

After a moment Lou said, "Yeah, I guess that's what women really like: to feel superior to the stronger sex." Then he added, "Even if it's only in the smallest possible way."

Liz gave a fake laugh, but good-humoredly. Another time she could have been repelled by his comment. But her spirits, boosted by this beautiful summer day and by the exhaustion of climbing the rocks—and by winning, of course—were way too great to take offense.

"No wonder you don't have a girlfriend, with that attitude of yours. You need to learn to treat women with style," she said, again observing Lou's reaction.

A smile toward the sky was his whole response. Lou looked like a perfectly happy man: never underestimate the effect of overexhaustion; together with sun and in the presence of a great girl it can easily become nirvana.

"No kidding, why don't you have a girlfriend?"

"You mean here on the island?" Lou said dryly.

"*No.*"

"The problem is I'm too happy with my life, that's why."

"*What?*"

"I just like to be sad sometimes. And if I had a girlfriend—with all these other things—I would be happy *all* the time."

Liz thought about it for a moment, then said, "You won't be happy all the time with a girlfriend," while brushing a strand of hair from her face.

21.

Jim and his younger brother, Andy, are in a gravel pit. By now it's early afternoon.

Jim was looking bored, holding a gun in his hands.

"Don't make a face like that," said Andy. "It's much more fun if you try to enjoy it a little."

Jim just closed his eyes and took a deep breath.

"Now try to hold it steady," said Andy with an energy and enthusiasm that only reduced Jim's willingness to enjoy it a little. "Do you hear me?"

"*Yes.*"

"*So do it,*" said Andy, while eyeing the thing critically. "Now hold your breath and aim at the target."

Jim did so. "And now?"

"Don't talk, damn it." Andy gave it another inspecting look. "Now pull the trigger."

A shot went off.

"You missed again." Andy walked a three-step circle, shaking his head, animated. "Let's try again."

"I'm not going to shoot this gun again. I promised I would try, and I'm done now," said Jim, looking at the bottles standing on top of an old log.

"Just try again. If you hit them it's so much fun."

"Maybe for you, but not for me."

"If you're determined to dislike it, you'll never enjoy it. You need to relax a little. You miss the whole point that way," said Andy, taking the gun.

He aimed.

Three shots went off.

Jim put his hands over his ears—but a little too late, it seemed.

Andy gave a pleased look at the three shattered bottles, readjusting his cowboy hat. He put the gun under his belt, then fingered a cigarette out of his breast pocket and lit it. "Damn it, you need to start living your life."

22.

Back on the sun-drenched island.

Lou was lying on top of the hill they had climbed, on his belly in the grass. Liz stood on a boulder, looking toward the horizon.

"It almost looks as if there's another island there," said Liz, trying to focus a little better while shielding her eyes from the sun with one hand.

Lou didn't say anything. He focused on a small plant that had come out of its seed. He probed it with his finger a little.

"What if it's the mainland?" said Liz.

An ant was climbing over the sprout. Lou was testing its footing by snapping the stem.

"If it's anything, it looks more like a small island, though. It's hard to tell."

Now he tested its wind endurance while blowing against it. The sprout tilted and the ant stopped a moment. Then the sprout swung back and the ant busily moved on.

"What are you doing?" said Liz, looking down at Lou.

"Nothing."

"What is it?"

"A sprout."

"What kind of sprout?" asked Liz.

"I don't know. Just a sprout," said Lou, poking it again with his finger.

Liz sat on the boulder. Then she jumped down to the grass by Lou and bent forward, taking a look at it herself.

"Do you know the *Pathfinder* mission they launched to Mars?" said Lou.

"You mean the satellite?"

"It was a ground mission, I believe. The interesting thing is they shot this package of steel and state-of-the-art technology to Mars. It landed there, and with the energy of some internal batteries it unfolded some solar panels. As the sun came up, the solar panels produced enough energy to unfold a ramp for the rover. The rover was inside the thing and drove out over the ramp to go—again with solar panels, I guess—on an excursion," said Lou, still looking at the sprout. "If you had the right technology, you could go on and on. You could program the mission to sustain and build itself. That way you could build whatever you wanted, under the stipulation that the rover can find the resources you need."

"Maybe you could, but one day they would run out of gas."

"No—they have solar panels."

"But they are limited."

"So you use the energy of the limited solar panels to build bigger ones," said Lou.

"It would never work."

"Of course, mankind will never be smart enough to pull it off, but theoretically it would work. With one small beginning package you could program it to build an empire." He stopped for a moment, blowing a little against the sprout. "That's what I always think of when I see a sprout. In a way it's the same. First there is the seed. In it is some limited energy and a lot of data. Then when it lands at the right place, it uses this energy to unfold itself; it builds a small root and two small solar panels."

Lou poked his finger against the two small leaves at the stem. Liz looked at it.

"These two solar panels start to produce energy. With this energy, the root starts to pump water and nutrition out of the soil. With these new resources the plant builds bigger solar panels and a bigger root system to get more energy and more resources," Lou said. "Isn't that crazy? Isn't that fantastic? And look at these two first panels. They will get shot down after the first real leaf is built. It's just good enough to start, but it's not really a leaf."

Liz looked at it a little longer, then moved close to the sprout and gave it a kiss. "You nice little sprout."

23.

Evening: Jim and his brother, Andy, stand next to a pickup truck in a dusty parking lot at a train station.

"This thing is slowly starting to grow over my head," said Jim, throwing a stone through the dust. "I mean, in the beginning it all seemed like a good idea. But are we really allowed to manipulate destiny? Do we really understand life well enough to know what's right and what's wrong? I wish we wouldn't have started with the whole thing."

"Come on!" said Andy. He was holding on to the open car door.

"Well, sometimes you have to let things be the way they are, even if you think you know how to improve them," said Jim. He was standing next to the rear wheel, looking over the lower sides of the truck toward the setting sun.

"Look," said Andy, "as I said before: We have to pull it off now. There is no other way. And besides, if you can improve something, why shouldn't you? Sometimes you have to help yourself. God helps those who help themselves."

"What worries me is that this improving business is exactly what brought me to this mess with my writing. That starts to worry me. If this exact same thing can mess up someone's writing, how can I be sure it can't mess up someone's life?" Jim said, and he reflected for a moment.

"Come on—it's hardly the same."

"Of course it is," said Jim, kicking the tire, looking at Andy. "If you really analyze it, it's exactly the same. I always wanted to improve something that didn't seem good enough. It's exactly the same if you really feel like thinking about it." Jim made a serious face toward the descending sun. "I listened to all these agents—that's the trouble. Do you know what they tell you? Do you want to know what crazy thing they tell you nowadays? They tell you to learn as much as possible about the best sellers of today. To basically make them one step better. They don't want you to make your own best thing. Just make something everyone already knows, and likes, a little better. It drives you crazy." He looked at the setting sun for a moment. "That was my whole trouble. I tried to become this perfect writer that can write best sellers like a machine. It's crazy but it's true. And if you don't follow the trend, and try to do your own thing, they look at you as if you're crazy."

He paused again, but this time looked to the ground. He stamped his shoe sole into the dust and looked at the pattern it created. Then, looking up again: "There are millions of beautiful things out there, and I'm such a moron and try to make up my own thing, *my improved thing.*" Jim looked for a beat to Andy, shaking his head slightly. "For example, just yesterday I saw this child with his mother getting off the bus. The mother had him by the hand and she nearly fell all over the sidewalk. And do you know why? Because the child was following a zigzag line on the asphalt and walked in front of the mother's feet. Isn't that beautiful?"

"I don't know. Yeah . . . I guess it is," Andy said, throwing a stone over the dust.

"You should have seen his big green eyes as his mother pulled him to her right. He didn't look up at her angrily, or surprised, or anxiously; just curiously. He probably thought it was only natural to walk along a zigzag line, since it's so much fun—I guess that's the way you think at that age," said Jim. "And stuff like this happens every day." He looked for a moment to the horizon. The setting sun cast a deep shadow on his face. "The problem is, you can't write stories about that stuff. No one really understands what you mean."

Andy didn't say anything; he was kicking dust with his boots. But it was clear he was listening.

"Like the other day in the subway," said Jim. "It was just too great. There was this musician playing the flute. Have you ever heard someone play the flute on the subway?"

"The flute? Heck, no."

"That's exactly the thing. It was the first time for me too. All of a sudden the train slowed down to a stop. And then, in the subway station, some construction workers were making a new platform. And while this guy was playing a pretty soft melody, a construction worker started to operate this pneumatic hammer. He was trying to lift the stone or something. But it didn't work the way he wanted it to. So he tried a little harder. He got pretty sore about it and started to jerk up and down with his hammer, right while the other guy was playing this terrific melody on his flute." Jim shook his head, remembering the scene. "But I think I was the only one in the whole car who saw it. Everyone else was just looking into space."

"Why don't you write about those things, then?" said Andy.

"What?"

"Why don't you write about those things?"

"*Why?* I'll tell you why. Because the problem is no one is interested in real life. No one is even interested while it's happening—why would they be interested if you wrote it down?"

"You could write a story about it, though."

"I could, but no one would care."

"Just make up a guy like you that runs around frustrated and can't believe all the great things that are running down the gutter. It would be funny." He threw another stone and laughed.

"You're so funny."

"It would be the perfect script. Just take your life. You'd only have to work out the details."

"Maybe it would. But no one would believe this other thing. It's just too fantastic," said Jim, scratching his head. "We never should have started it." Now he shook his head slightly. "I can't believe you put a new one there."

"What should I have done?"

"I distinctly said it must be a rusty one. I know I distinctly said it. A new one is asking for trouble," said Jim.

"How do you get the bastard all rusty if it's perfectly new?"

"I don't know," said Jim. "There are ways."

"So tell me *these ways*."

"I don't know. Pee over it and leave it out overnight."

"Not with the steel of today. You can't even get lousy tools these days. That's the trouble. Everything is stainless steel today."

A train was coming in, slowing down at the deserted train station.

Jim turned his head. "That's my train. I really have to run now. Good-bye . . . and give my regards to your new girlfriend—what's her name again? Ma . . . Max . . . ?"

"Maxilla."

"Maxilla. Yes," Jim said, and started to walk. Then he turned his head and said over his shoulder, "So we do everything as discussed. And thanks for driving me back to the train station. I appreciate it."

Andy looked after him for a moment as he walked away, then got in his truck. He started the engine, turned on the music, and accelerated through the dusty parking lot toward the street.

24.

On the island. About the same time.

"That was a great day, just exploring the island, doing nothing," said Lou, lying on his back on a stone.

They were on top of a small cliff. Liz was looking over the edge, down the fifteen-foot waterfall. "Do you think we can jump down when we go back?"

"Of course we could. It's not that high, but our clothes would get wet, and it's not that warm anymore."

"We can throw our clothes down first. Let's do it." Liz started to take off her sweater. It was the gray one with the hood—the only piece of clothing she had beside her bikini.

"I don't have any bathing suit," said Lou.

"So jump naked. What's the big deal?"

"No big deal. But you jump naked too," said Lou, challenging her.

"I was just going to," said Liz, while slipping off her bikini. "Come on, it's your turn."

She looked at Lou, then jumped down, shrieking.

Lou kept lying on the stone. For a moment he looked to the evening sky. He shivered a little, then got up.

Liz was swimming in the pool, looking up. *"Lou!"*

He couldn't hear her over the noise of the waterfall. By the time Lou stood at the edge Liz was swimming again. He observed her for a moment.

"What's up? You're still wearing your clothes," Liz shouted as she spotted him.

He disappeared without a word behind the edge.

"Lou?"

After a moment he came running over the edge.

Liz, startled, shouted, *"Whoa!"*

He surfaced after a suspended period under water, but he couldn't do so without a smile on his face. Then: "Brrr . . . it's freezy."

"Only the first moment. Isn't it beautiful here?"

"It certainly is," he said, and splashed water toward her.

She dived.

All of a sudden Lou disappeared, as if some force from below had pulled him down.

25.

Andy on the cell phone, still riding back in his pickup truck.

"Take it easy," said Andy. "I told you about fifty times it's all going according to plan."

He listened for a moment to the receiver. "Yeah, I know."

He listened again.

"Look. I'm going to call you tomorrow, and you will see everything is perfectly all right. I mean wh—"

He listened.

"Yes, I know, but just tell me, why shouldn't everything be all right?"

26.

On the island. A couple of minutes later.

Lou was shivering, sitting on a stone in his underpants.

"We definitely stayed in this cold water too long," he said.

Liz sat next to him, rubbing his arms. "You poor thing."

Lou turned and lay stomach-down on the warm stone. Still shivering, he said, "I always was the first to get cold in the water. I don't know what it is." After a moment he added, "You didn't believe me that I sink if I don't move. Right to the bottom. Did you?"

"It's natural. Everyone does."

"No. You didn't," he said.

"I did when I exhaled all the air."

"Yes, but I do even if I have my lungs all filled up," he

said. "I mean, I showed it to you. You have to admit, that's pretty interesting."

"I guess all men do," she said, looking at his underpants.

"No, they don't. We once tested it in school. I was the only one who went down."

"Where did you get those underpants?" Liz asked, still looking at them.

"Why?"

"They look old-fashioned."

"I like them," Lou said, still shivering on the warm stone.

"Where did you get them?"

"Why?"

"I'm just interested to know . . . Why, is it a big secret or something?"

"It's not. But you have to admit, they are kind of stylish."

Liz gave them a critical look, then lightly slapped him on the buttocks.

"Hey, what's that for?" Lou protested.

Liz giggled and gave them another inspection. "They even have a hole in them."

"I don't mind a small hole in my underpants. Especially if they're my favorite underpants. What kind of an owner of underpants would I be if I just threw them away after all we've been through?" he said, and pretended to dwell on good memories.

"Where did you get them, though?" Liz stressed.

"First you have to admit that they're pretty cool."

"Okay. They are pretty cool," she said.

"You didn't mean it."

"No, because I think they are old-fashioned."

"I'm not going to tell you where I got my underpants from if you insult them."

"You're crazy," she said, still looking at the underpants.

Lou didn't say anything; he just flexed his buttocks.

Liz giggled.

"Don't you have favorite underpants?" Lou asked.

"I don't know . . . Where did you get them?"

"From my grandfather. I inherited them."

Liz laughed, still looking at them. "That's what they look like," she said, and pulled them down a little.

"It's time to go now," said Lou, rolling his eyes. "It's impossible to speak with you about underpants." He got up, giving his underpants a pleased look.

27.

At the Fraziers' home. Jim arrives home from his trip to his brother's.

"How's Uncle Andy?" asked Pete as Jim came in.

"Fine, as always. You know his energy—his *ideas*," said Jim.

"What's wrong with his ideas?" asked Pete.

"Nothing, why?"

"Just the way you said it," said Pete.

"Nothing's wrong. I'm just a little tired from the trip, that's all. How was your day?"

"Just the usual."

28.

Back on the island.

It was slowly getting dark. Liz and Lou were walking back, following the small river.

"No kidding—did they really once belong to your grandfather?"

"If you mean my underpants, yes. But if you don't like them, I don't want to talk about it."

"Why don't you buy new ones?" said Liz.

"I told you—I like them the way they are."

"Yeah, but you can get the exact same— What's this?" said Liz, looking to the ground.

Lou turned. "Looks like a saw."

Liz squatted down, looking at it. Then she looked around; she didn't see anything but dark forest. "That's strange. Isn't it?"

Lou kept looking at the saw, frowning.

"What's it supposed to mean?" said Liz.

"I don't know. It's a saw. And it looks new."

"Strange. Isn't it? Does this mean there are people on this island?" said Liz, with a little fear in her voice.

"I don't know," said Lou. "It can't have been here more than a couple of days. It would rust in no time, with the salt in the air."

"I'm afraid. Let's go back—it's getting really dark," said Liz.

"There must be a logical explanation, though."

"Yes—there are people around."

Lou looked at her, then back at the saw. He blinked a couple of times. "Let's go," he said. "We'll go back and take the saw with us."

They made their way through the dark forest in silence, but it was obvious that they walked unusually fast and close together. All of the sudden the island wasn't what it had been a minute ago.

29.

If there is a break in the theater, it's now, and it's a short one.

part three

30.

The next morning: Jim's walking down a street, probably on his way to work. The sky is clear blue, like it is on a nice summer morning.

"*What?*" he almost shouted into his cell phone.

"They're building a raft," repeated Andy. He was sitting on his deck, drinking his outdoor morning coffee.

"What does that mean?"

"I don't know. But it looks like they plan to leave," said Andy. "Maybe they got scared by the thunderstorm last night."

"That means trouble! . . . That means trouble. Did they find the saw?"

"Yes."

"*Damn*, I knew it! What should they think if they find a perfectly new saw on—" Jim exhaled some air instead of finishing his sentence. Then he swung his cell phone through the air and shouted, "Moron!" to a passing taxi that had just cut a turn too close.

Andy kept listening to his phone, a little puzzled. He took a sip of his coffee.

"Look," he said, once he knew he had Jim back on the line, "they probably saw the other island. The one I observe them from. Maybe they think it's the mainland."

"What can we do?"

"Worst-case scenario is that they leave and head for that island. Nothing can happen—no harm's done."

"Yes, but what can we do? We can't just pick them up there, can we?"

"No—heck, no."

"We have to do something," said Jim, waiting by a Don't Walk sign.

"Look, let's observe what they're doing. Maybe they're just building the raft for fishing—who knows?"

"I don't like it, but I guess that's the only thing we can do now. It was a crazy idea from the beginning."

"It's not crazy. I told you—it's likely to work out, because she just went through some split-up with a good-looking, lazy, boring bastard. Beautiful women need someone who understands their beauty." Andy stopped for a moment. "Not only their physical beauty. You know what I mean, don't you?"

"*Yeah, yeah, yeah.*"

"So let's sleep on it. Nothing's out of control. I'll keep an eye on them."

Jim thought for a moment. "But call me as soon as something happens."

"Of course I will . . . Oh, I almost forgot—did you see the commercial yet?"

"You mean your new one? . . . No."

"Check the Discovery Channel—it's on all the time. It came off better than expected. It's really great."

"That's great for you."

31.

Jim is on his way home. He's walking to the subway station with Arnold.

"What would you do if you got lost on a beautiful island with a beautiful girl?" asked Jim.

"That would be great . . . What would I do, though?" He started to think. "What do you mean, what would I do, Mr. Frazier?" he said, looking up at Jim.

"Just tell me what you would do."

Arnold started to think again. "Well, I wouldn't have to do anything, because there the girl's almost forced to fall in love with me. That would be great," said Arnold.

"But what if you got scared on the island at night?"

"Hmm. That's a good question." He thought for a moment, then said, "I would probably build a fort where I could live."

"That's an interesting idea," said Jim, pressing his lips together. "But what if you had enough wood to build a raft?"

"You can't just build a raft. You need tools."

"So if you had the tools?"

"Then I would probably build a raft," said Arnold, but it seemed he had already forgotten what he would build it for.

Jim realized it was a hopeless case, so they walked in silence for a while.

32.

At the Fraziers'. Evening.

Pete was glued to the TV set.

All of a sudden he stood up and said, "Whoa, that's awesome."

He sat down again. "Whoa, that's really something." Then, "Mom?"

No answer came.

The door opened and Jim came in.

"Hi, Dad. Did you see the commercial yet? It was just on."

Jim was looking around, trying to get his bearings.

33.

On the phone. Next morning.

"*What?*"

"They left the island," repeated Andy. He almost had to shout over the loud hip-hop music in his car.

"Where are they now?" asked Jim.

"Probably on the way to the other island. I just saw them leave."

"This thing's slowly driving me crazy," said Jim.

"Just think it all through. It's no big deal," said Andy.

"*No big deal?* It all started with this crazy saw idea. Your preaching how important it is to have a saw and all," said Jim. "Beth and the kids are starting to ask questions. They feel that something is wrong with me. How can I act as if everything is all right if it isn't?"

"Just tell them you're a little nervous because you're having trouble with your new book again," said Andy.

"But it looks good, I told you—for the first time it looks good. Yesterday I really got an agent excited about this new idea. It doesn't necessarily mean a lot, but she got really excited about the idea. I just have to pull it through without getting sidetracked again this time, that's all."

"They don't need to know that. Just think it through. Just tell them you're going through a difficult time because you're having trouble with your book."

"But I already told them it looks good."

"So tell Beth and the kids that the agent changed her mind—nowadays everything is unpredictable."

"I'll think about it, but we have to do something."

"Yes, we have to wait and see. They may have just left for the other island and everything is all right."

"Maybe. Maybe you're right. Maybe you're not. I need to think. I guess it's best if you keep observing them. Just let me know if something happens. I mean, what else can we do?"

34.

Afternoon. Pete walks along a street with two other kids.

"And then, when it starts to lower the thing, it almost kills you," said one kid.

"Man, if I had a favorite commercial, this would be it," said the third kid.

"I can't believe your uncle made it."

"He didn't make it," said Pete. "He just gave them the idea."

35.

On the phone. Evening.

"They're on the other island now?" said Jim into the phone. Sitting at home in an easy chair. "At least that's good news. What are they doing on the island?"

"It's hard to tell. They basically just arrived."

Jim looked around the living room to the open doors. No one seemed to be around, but he kept his voice down and the receiver close. "The one thing we have to be concerned about is that they don't spot you."

"That's no problem," said Andy. "I know what I'm doing."

"What makes me a little uneasy is the shark that killed that boy. It wasn't too far from where they are," said Jim, switching the channels on the TV set. "Did you hear the news?"

"*Did I hear the news!* You have to be dead or some crazy bastard living in the woods not to hear it," said Andy. "But there's nothing to worry about. I mean, they make a big deal over nothing. It's just a shark frenzy, straight out of *Jaws.*"

"Obviously it killed a boy, though," said Jim, again looking attentively around.

"Do you know how many boys get killed, *daily,* on

their bicycles? They don't make the news. But a single shark attack—they even broadcast it on CNN."

"It's the fascination of beast against mankind. It's not the same as someone dying on a bicycle."

"Maybe it isn't. But maybe it is. Let's discuss this another time. I really have to get out of here," said Andy. "Take it easy now—everything will be fine."

36.

The next morning at the Fraziers', just before Pete has to leave for school.

Pete sat on the sofa watching TV. He had a glass of milk in his hand. On the small table in front of him was a bowl of cereal.

Next to him sat Sarah, eating a piece of bread. This time Pete was the one interested in watching TV.

"Hey, Pete, Mom and I are going to the beach today," said Sarah.

"So what?"

"And my friend Salina is coming along."

"I see."

"We're going to learn to swim."

"Okay, can I watch TV now?"

Sarah had finished her bread and stood on the sofa now. She started to jump up and down.

"*Doiiing. Doiiing. Doiiing.*"

Pete didn't care. He kept watching TV.

But Sarah had another idea. Every time she jumped she said, "I'm going to the beach. I'm going to the beach . . ."

That did the job.

"*Okay! Okay!* I'm trying to watch TV here. Either sit down and shut up or leave me alone."

Sarah stopped jumping and looked at Pete. "You're such a moron. You're just jealous," she said, then jumped down from the sofa and ran out of the room.

37.

Jim and Arnold walk through the city, going to work.

"How did it turn out with your new book idea?" Arnold asked.

"It got declined," said Jim. He looks older than the last time we saw him.

"*What?* But you said—"

"I know."

"*But*—"

"They changed their minds, that's all," said Jim.

Arnold thought about it for a moment, then looked up at Jim. He saw Jim's tired face and looked at the ground. "What are you going to do now, Mr. Frazier?"

"I don't know. I really don't know," said Jim, pressing his lips together. "What would you do in my position?"

"*Me?* Hmm. I don't know. I'm not a writer. I was never really good at writing essays and stuff."

"It can be a real advantage, not believing in something."

"But . . . but you told me—"

"I know. Maybe I was wrong. I don't know," Jim said, looking into space. "Maybe I'm just a little confused, though."

Arnold didn't know what to say, so he just kept looking at the ground, thinking.

"Do you have a brother, Arnold?"

"No, a sister," Arnold said, rolling his eyes.

Jim saw it and smiled a little. "My brother told me about a friend of his, who isn't exactly a psychiatrist, just someone who really understands life and helps other people out. He told me I should go visit him." Jim stopped and thought for a moment. "Would you think I was crazy if I went to a psychiatrist, Arnold?"

Arnold was looking up at Jim, smiling. "I know you're not crazy, Mr. Frazier."

"Thank you, Arnold. You have a good mind. Did anyone ever tell you that?"

Pride crossed Arnold's face. He seemed to consider it. He moved his head a little from side to side, and his lower lip started to protrude. "No. No one ever told me that, Mr. Frazier," he said, looking up at Jim with big eyes.

38.

Early evening. We see Jim talking to an elderly person but we can't hear them. Instead we are listening to music.

Jim sat on a chair talking to an old man sitting behind a desk. The arrangement of the room indicated that this was the psychiatrist Jim had been talking about. The old man didn't quite look like a psychiatrist, though. He just looked rather weird.

The old man's movements were deliberate and full of motivation, and Jim's . . . well . . . he seemed to have retreated into himself, cursing either his brother's *great* ideas or his own stupidity in following them.

Judging by the way they moved, it was clear that the old man was full of motivation, . . . and Jim . . . *well* . . . his motivation seemed rather *moderate*.

39.

In another place at the same time.

Pete was sitting with a couple of friends in front of the TV. He checked his watch. "According to my watch, it must be on . . . now."

Everyone grew silent, staring at the TV.

A big John Deere appears in a deserted landscape. It's one of the last great machines—with eight huge tires and a motor that roars like an explosion—that blows everyone's mind. Music with a heavy beat starts to set in. The John Deere's engine starts. Smoke is shooting out of the exhaust pipe.

While the John Deere shifts into gear and starts to roll, the sound becomes more intense. To see this machine in a picture is one thing, but to see it in action is pure madness.

Everything is rolling with great momentum now, the music and the John Deere. The tension is high.

Then the refrain of the song sets in, and the John Deere lowers the fork into the soil, dragging it with great force through the landscape. Fog is lifting; everything is powerful. Total craziness.

After a moment we see the crew that filmed the commercial, totally excited, jumping around, giving the thumbs-up and high fives. There are some girls in bikinis.

A sentence appears on the screen: "Farming never gets boring."

For a short moment we see the John Deere pulling the fork a little farther toward the horizon.

Pete and his friends, still glued to the screen, were all hypnotically smiling.

40.

We are back with Jim and the old man behind the desk.

"Life is a game. It's a book and it's a movie, Mr. Frazier," said the old man presently, starting to nod his head.

Jim gave the old man a suspicious look, seeming surprised that it wasn't just a family saying.

The old man didn't notice it, though. He was still nodding his head.

"That's exactly what I've been saying," said Jim. "But what if you don't agree with the narrator anymore?"

"Why don't you write about it, Mr. Frazier?" said the old man. He had stopped with the annoying nodding, but now he was speaking in a calm, warm, comforting way, as though appealing to an eight-year-old. "It helps a great deal to write things down, to sort it out, Mr. Frazier. Sometimes you find something pretty confusing and you can't understand it, but then you write everything down and you realize it wasn't even a problem. You realize you just weren't looking at it the right way. You don't even have to be a writer. I give this advice to everyone. I even do it myself."

Jim rolled his eyes. He seemed to have relaxed a little by now—maybe he even started to see a certain irony in the old man.

"As a matter of fact," said the old man, raising his eyebrows, "I just told it to the gentleman that was in here before you. He is depressed, and I told him to write about it. I said, 'Write down everything you can figure out about the problem, while focusing on the positive side.'" The old man stopped and smiled at Jim, probably still animated by his train of thought.

"How can you write about depression focusing on the positive side?"

"You can, you can," the old man said, nodding again, still smiling.

Jim took a deep breath.

"Try to figure out how you felt before. You know, before the unhappiness. Then try to figure out where the excitement about life has gone. Where it is hiding, in other words. What made it leave in the first place? If you really understand these things, you may be able to track it down and get it back, Mr. Frazier."

Jim was looking at the floor. "The problem is you can't sell stuff like this. Today you have to write what they want to hear," he said, looking the old man directly in the eye. "That's how it is *today*. It's crazy—but that's how it is."

"I didn't mean to say you should write about it to sell it," said the old man, smiling kindly toward Jim. "Write it down for *yourself*. You have to express yourself to get to know yourself. If you write down your thoughts, Mr. Frazier, you build something up. It's almost like a hill from where you have a better perspective. The more you write, the more you climb this hill and the better your perspective gets." For a moment it was silent. The old man seemed to be thinking. He started to rap the desk with a pen.

"Well, Mr. Frazier," he started again, "maybe now that I think about it, you *could* write about your life professionally. In my opinion, the best writers did nothing other than pack their own problems into little stories. *That's* what makes the stories good in the first place."

"Maybe if you've had a really interesting life or an experience, but none of the things that have happened to *me* seem like good stories. They almost look made up," said Jim.

"Heck, no. *No*. These things are definitely not dreamed up," said the old man, highly animated. "It's pure life. It's pure life," he mumbled for a moment. "Find a made-up story. They're always about some boxer having a hell of an uphill battle until he beats the crap out of the bad guy in the final match. Or it's about some couple getting lost on some small island, first hating each other's guts, then falling in love."

Jim started a little and gave the old man a suspicious look again, just a little longer this time.

"Okay, I've got to run now. Thanks a lot. I appreciate your advice," he said, and got up.

41.

Later that evening. It was getting dark, with huge clouds built up on the horizon. A single pickup truck was speeding through the deserted landscape.

"They must have left the island. I couldn't spot them, and the raft is gone," said Andy into the cell phone, driving his truck. "Maybe they left for the third island. Maybe they thought it was the mainland."

The truck sped on.

42.

By now it's dark and raining.

Jim stood at the side of the street. He held a thumb out. A car stopped.

43.

In the living room at the Fraziers'.

Pete was watching TV. Beth came in.

"Hi, Pete. Isn't Dad home yet?"

"Nope. He called. He won't be home till late."

Rain was slashing against the windows of the living room.

"Are you kidding me?" said Beth, looking toward the dark glass. "He doesn't have to work late at the supermarket."

"He said it's something to do with his book deal. I guess he had to leave town. I didn't ask."

"In this weather?" said Beth, shaking her head. "He and his books. He needs to realize no one wants to publish his books."

44.

The wiper was working its way over the windshield, removing the smashed raindrops.

"I love driving at night. Don't you?"

The car kept speeding over the wet street, fragments of a yellow line zipping by.

"I'm not too good a driver. Actually, I don't have a car," said Jim.

"Isn't it cozy inside, with the rain pouring down? I wouldn't want to be out there right now," said the young woman, looking at the reflection of an oncoming headlight. "But inside here it's nice, isn't it?"

The oncoming car zoomed by, splashing water on the left side of their car.

Jim looked over at her.

She wore a white fur hat. Her brown hair came nicely to below her ears.

"Yes, it is," said Jim. "I'm really glad you picked me up."

"I pick up hitchhikers a lot. It must be horrible waiting in the cold, dark rain," she said, and thought for a moment. "Sometimes I feel like being alone, though. Then I don't pick them up."

"I take it you drive a lot?"

"Sometimes I drive a lot, sometimes I don't."

Jim reflected for a moment, thinking of something to say. He looked around a little, then started to move his hand over the side window, removing the fog.

The young woman looked over at him.

Jim was looking out the window now.

She focused back on the street.

After a moment Jim got bored with looking out the window. He probably couldn't see anything anyway—it was too dark. He rubbed his hands for a second, tried to look content, and wiggled himself a little into the seat. "It's really messy out there," he said conversationally.

The woman didn't say anything. She was focused on the road.

Jim looked at her, then out the windshield. The wiper cleared his side of the windshield a little, and then it started to get blurry again. Then the wiper came by again.

"Driving in the car reminds me of my father—that's why I like it," she said. "He's dead now."

A small pause followed.

"I'm sorry to hear it."

"He had cancer," she said. "Do you know anyone who had cancer?"

"My grandfather, but I didn't know him."

"If you lose someone that fast, you start to realize just how much you loved them."

"I'm sure you do. It must be intense," said Jim.

"It is. It's like getting hit with a stone. It shakes you so hard, you lose orientation. I was shattered and sad for a long time," said the woman, and she thought about it. "But in another way, it's like waking up." She started to fiddle around with the defroster. Then she tested with her hand to see if the hot air was reaching the windshield. She seemed to be shaking a little. "Do you want to listen to the radio?" she said, and started to turn the radio on, trying to find a good frequency. She listened a little to the music, then said, "Do you want a cigarette?" fingering one out for herself.

"No, thank you."

"Ah," she said, and put her cigarette back into the box.

"But you have one if you feel like it," said Jim. "I really don't mind."

"Thank you, but it's not that important."

They drove on in silence for a while. Jim looked out the side window. Now and then they passed a house; otherwise it was just trees and bushes.

"We used to spend *days* in the car, my father and me. We drove back and forth to Mexico. My father came from Mexico."

"Oh, really?" said Jim.

"We always brought old cars and other old stuff with us. Some things he gave to our relatives—other things he sold. He was quite a handyman. He could fix everything. In Mexico—he even built a house by himself."

"Is your mother Mexican too? You don't look Mexican."

"She's American. Sometimes she came with us, sometimes she didn't."

For a minute or two they drove on in silence.

Jim rubbed his left index finger for a while.

"Do you mind if I turn down the heat a notch?" said the woman.

"No. Not at all. It's really getting a little hot in here," said Jim.

"Do you have a family?"

The question caught Jim off guard.

"Yes," he said, after a moment. "Yes, I do."

"I guess it isn't too easy being a father," said the woman, and smiled a little. "I mean, it must be difficult to understand a daughter sometimes—or a son." She focused on the windshield wipers for a moment. "But sometimes it's pretty hard to understand fathers too."

Jim was looking to the radio display.

"We had this terrific fight when I was sixteen. I left the house and never spoke a word to him again," said the woman. "Not until he was deadly sick in the hospital. He was one of those guys who go to the doctor only when they can't stand the pain anymore. The cancer was all over the place by then."

It became silent again in the car. The only remaining sounds came from the radio, and the beating of the rain-drops . . . and the noise of the tires on the wet road.

"We're almost there—maybe two more miles. Are you familiar with the roads around here?"

"Not really."

"After you drop me off, just stay on this street for about another mile and it will lead you right back to the highway."

"Good." The woman pressed the automatic lighter.

After a while the lighter popped out and she pulled a cigarette out of the box and lit it. She took a couple of drags. "During his last weeks in the hospital we became friends again. But we never *really* talked to each other."

She took another drag of the cigarette.

"But now there's so much I have to tell him."

For a moment she looked at the windshield. It wasn't clear if she was looking just at the glass or through it.

Jim slid his left hand under his thigh and started to massage the muscle.

"Whenever I drive the car at night, I feel like he's with me, and like he understood why I did what I did."

The car kept speeding on, the rain slashing down.

The woman tapped the ash off her cigarette, then took a deep drag. For a moment she seemed to be absorbed by something, then slowly let out the smoke.

"You can drop me off at the next corner," said Jim. He was trying to focus into the distance.

After a moment he said, "Right there," pointing toward an open spot on the shoulder of the street.

"Are you sure?" She looked at Jim.

"Yes."

The car stopped and Jim got out.

He looked back in. "Thanks a lot," he said. "You saved my day." He started to close the door, but he stopped. "You're a great woman. Your father must have known it." He closed the door and started to walk through the rain.

The car turned and sped away.

Jim started to walk faster. Then he started to run.

Another car came from the opposite direction, casting shadows on his body. The light became brighter. Then the car zoomed by, leaving a wake of spray behind.

45.

Jim rapped on the door of the house, then barged in.

Andy sat in the middle of the room in an easy chair. Placed in front of him was a small table with a steering wheel on it.

Andy jerked another turn, then pushed some buttons, and the noise of tires and music faded to a flowing beat. "You were fast. How did you make it that quick?" he said, then turned in his seat, looking at Jim. "Whoa, what happened? You're soaked."

Jim walked—almost stumbled—toward the fireplace and sat on a chair.

"You need something dry. Damn, what's going on outside?" said Andy, getting up.

After a moment he came back into the room and threw some dry clothes toward Jim. "How did you make it that quick, anyway?"

Jim pulled his shirt over his head, still breathing heavily. "If this is a dream, wake me up." Jim shook his head. "It's crazy." He put the wet shirt on the mantel. "Do you remember the old saying 'Life is a movie and it's a book'?"

"Of course."

"As I was running to your house, it was haunting my mind. And I couldn't get it out," Jim said, and slipped down his pants.

"Running?"

"Just from the corner. I hitchhiked."

Andy took the wet pants and the shirt from the mantel and walked out of the room. He came back with a towel.

"I personally never believed there was much wisdom in that saying," said Jim. "I mean, all I thought it meant was that whenever you're in trouble, if you keep looking hard enough, you'll find a way." Jim put the dry pants on, then took the towel. "But as I was running through the rain, I realized you don't really need a saying to understand that, do you? That's basically clear to everyone anyway."

"True, you don't need a saying for that," confirmed Andy.

"I guess the saying can give you energy to *keep trying* to find a way," said Jim absently while rubbing his hair dry. "But anyway, what I couldn't get off my mind was the idea that someone was behind all these things in my life. Someone that takes a lot of pleasure in putting me into these very strange situations. What if God and his friends put me into these situations and now they're having a hell of a time watching how I behave; if I'm strong enough, if I stumble, if I feel awkward, if I say what I think . . . It may be a lot of fun for them, but it's not for me," said Jim. "What if the saying were true in the literal meaning? It would totally make sense with my life. It's scary." He stopped rubbing his hair and looked at Andy. "What could you do about it then? How could you

escape their attention and lead a halfway normal life?"
He started to rub his hair again, looking worried and
tired.

Andy was looking at Jim and started to smile. "You're
just going through a difficult time, that's all. And even if
it were true, even if someone put us into these situations,
it wouldn't change a thing. You still have control of
everything. And do you know why?"

Jim was looking at Andy.

"I'll tell you why, damn it. You are a writer. You
should know it best. You can't just take *someone* and put
them into a loser's situation—it doesn't work. Yes, you
could do it in a book, but something would seem wrong.
It would come off as false. And do you know why?
Because a situation has to fit the character. My character,
for example, wouldn't work in a pathetic situation—I'm
a fighter. So if there's someone behind my story, he can
use me only in that way," said Andy. "You yourself write
the book. If you want to change the script, change your
character. Is that really so hard to see?" He shook his
head for a beat. "What happens if you put a guy full of
self-pity and a guy that tackles life like a panther into the
same situation? Does the story end the same way?"

"No."

"You're right. It's not the same story. You need a
weak guy, someone that gives in fast, someone that gets
sore about everything, in a loser story. And you need
someone that jumps at life with excitement, someone

that never gives in, someone with ideas, in a winner story . . . You need a mean guy to be hated, and you need a guy with integrity to be loved."

Jim was now looking at Andy.

"Those are the rules. In writing—*and life*. I guess they teach this stuff in writing school, or if they don't, they should."

Jim kept looking at Andy for a while. "Let's get the boat and get them back." Then he said, "We can't waste time."

Music starts to play, and we float over the surface of the ocean.

46.

The water is calm and peaceful, and the sun is shining through some light mist; it must be morning. With a picture like this on the screen, one just wants to take a breath of the fresh air.

We approach a raft floating on the surface of the water.

We cut to Lou and Liz on the handmade raft. Liz is sitting on the edge, letting her legs dangle into the water. Lou is sitting against the pole in the middle of the raft, looking in the opposite direction.

"I was once on vacation, with a friend," said Liz. "And we ate only ice cream for the entire week. That's about all. Girls don't do stuff like that all the time." She started to stir the water with her legs, looking down.

"Uncle Andy says that's healthy."

"Who's Uncle Andy?"

"My father's brother. He has these crazy ideas all the time. He lives from his ideas, basically. He sells them," said Lou. "He also eats only ice cream for a couple of days sometimes. Do you know why?"

Liz had stopped looking down at her circling feet for a moment and was now looking over her shoulder to Lou. "Because he likes it?"

"For one thing, he probably likes it," said Lou, rubbing the back of his head against the pole. "But he also believes that that way the body starts to appreciate normal food again. He thinks the body can know what healthy food is only if it knows what unhealthy food is. And if you give your body only the most tender treatment, it gets spoiled and takes it for granted. But if you sometimes give it something to cope with—like eating only ice cream for a couple of days, I guess—then it starts to deal with it and begins to appreciate normal food again."

"It's possible. We didn't get sick on the vacation. We didn't even gain weight," Liz said, and pushed down on the wood with her arms, observing how her side of the raft sank a little then came up again.

"He also says it's healthy to get drunk once in a while. Just to give the body something to think about. He always has these opinions. He used to kid my father because he hates cold water. Uncle Andy said no *body* likes cold water, but that you shouldn't care. Just jump in and look how the bastard reacts—that's the way he talks," said Lou, amused. "He says if you treat your body only with great care, it gets lazy. And a lazy body causes you pain all the time, since it knows it can manipulate you that way to keep comfortable."

"In a way, he's probably right. It sounds sort of extreme, though," said Liz. She lifted her feet out of the water, touching them to gauge their temperature. Then she put one foot next to the other and covered them with her hands.

"He says depressed people don't treat their bodies like that. Depressed people try to keep their bodies comfortable. That's the whole trouble, Andy says. He has so many opinions, it's almost like a religion—some crazy religion, though," Lou said, and turned his head to see what Liz was doing.

She didn't see him look. She was still warming her feet.

47.

"We're late. It's already nine," said Jim with concern.

They were coming out of the shrubby landscape, a small, sandy beach in front of them. There were two boats lying stranded in the sand. They walked toward them.

"All right," said Andy, squatting down to the sand.

He drew a circle in the sand. "This is the island we're on." Now he drew a long line. "This here is the mainland." He made two other small circles. "These are the other islands." He looked at the sketched-out map for a moment. "I guess we'll find them somewhere in between." He made a cross on one of the smaller islands. "Here is where they started, so we'll start there too. You go west, I go east. We scan the whole area. If we can't find them here we go farther out to the ocean." He drew an arrow in the sand between the mainland and the islands. "If they tried to come to the mainland, the current probably drifted them west. Without a motor, you can't make it. So in the worst case we look for them in this area." He drew another circle. "Let's say we start now and meet at noon. If we find them, great; if not, we'll make further plans. Any questions?"

Jim was eyeing the drawings for a moment longer. "What do we tell them if we find them?"

"Hmm? That's a good question."

"I guess we can't tell them the truth?"

"No, hell, no, not the truth. In a way, no one knows what really happened. So why not just tell them that they were missed, so we started looking for them?"

"But they may wonder why we're searching on our own without help. I mean, it sounds kind of careless not to inform the authorities," said Jim.

"That's another point to consider," mused Andy. "Why not tell them that we found them by accident?"

"You mean, as if we were just speeding over the ocean for our own amusement, and then by chance we found them?" said Jim, looking at Andy.

"All right, that's out of the question. Look, we can solve that problem when the time comes. Right now we shouldn't waste precious time. We should try to focus on finding them. Let's say the one who finds them improvises something. I guess we have time to think about that before we spot them."

They started to pull the boats into the water. Andy started the engine and sped off first.

48.

We are back with Liz and Lou. We see them both on their raft. Lou is lying on his back, and Liz is sitting against the pole, looking toward him.

"And the crazy thing is, we didn't even realize it," said Lou. "But what happened to that guy in the book I told you about happens to everyone one way or another." He looked at the sky for a moment. "Whatever problems you had as a kid you naturally try to fight. You may think that it's all a mess once in a while, but step by step you will find a way out, and you learn and grow a lot." He shook his head slightly. "That's the beauty of life." A look of awe crossed his face. "Heck, life always finds a way. You can't imprison life."

"Yes, you can," said Liz, observing Lou's reaction.

He didn't move; he just kept looking up at the sky.

"I was once on vacation somewhere, and at the hotel they had this aquarium in the lobby. One day I noticed a little fish in the tank looking at the glass. There were many different fish in the tank, but only one like him. So I got pretty close in front of him and looked back in, to try to get his attention. But he didn't move. He just looked at the glass. A day later I passed the tank again, and this fish was still in the same spot, looking at the glass. The other fish, which weren't unique, chased each other all over the place. But he only looked at the glass." Liz reflected for a moment. "Isn't that sad?"

"That was just because he was in captivity. In nature he would never have given up looking for someone of his kind. Even if he never managed to find one," Lou said. "And as long as he was looking, he would never feel blue."

49.

Jim was already back by the small lagoon, looking toward the water. After a moment he heard some noise, then he spotted Andy closing in on his boat.

Andy came full bore toward the sand, pulling up the engine shortly before hitting the shore. He leaned backward so as not to tumble forward with the impact. The momentum delivered him about five yards inland, right next to Jim.

Finally stopped, he stood and eyed Jim critically, pressing his lips together. "Nothing?"

Jim shook his head. "No."

"Did you cover your whole area?"

"Twice."

"Me too."

"Let's go out to the ocean, then," said Jim.

50.

We see the same small lagoon. No one is there. The sun is now orange and almost touching the water.

After a moment the shapes of two boats appear against the sunlight. They are closing in on the sand. This time neither of the boats hits with much enthusiasm. Each figure gets out, and we observe,

*by slowly turning our perspective, how they walk
through the sand back to the trail. This time it's just
a dark spot between the shrubs. They enter the darkness and disappear.*

51.

*With a cut we float over the surface of the ocean. It
must be just about daybreak of the next morning. A
warm breeze blows over the water, the way it sometimes does in the summer before a thunderstorm. The
sky, reflected on the surface, seems gray and cloudy.*

*We keep floating over the water for a while. After
a minute or two the camera raises up and we see the
cloudy horizon above the sea.*

We float a little longer.

*All of a sudden we see something on the horizon.
We are way too far away to tell what it really is—it's
just that we see it's the shape of* something.

We float a little closer.

With a cut the screen turns black.

*We're listening to the wind for a while. We also
hear someone breathing.*

*Eyes open and we see the cloudy sky. On the right
side of the screen we see long brown hair moving in
the morning breeze. It almost looks like Liz's hair.*

From here on, everything happens slowly.

"Do you think they will find us?" It was Liz's voice we heard. She sounded exhausted.

"I don't know," said Lou. He also sounded exhausted.

"It looks like rain," said Liz.

A long moment of silence.

"I always used to go running when it rained. Always through the forest," said Lou. "Have you ever gone running in the rain?"

"No."

"You have to. It's the best thing you can do. If you run through the woods while it rains, all the colors are so beautiful. Everything shines. Everything is green as hell."

A small pause.

"In a way, rain is nothing more than Mother Nature bringing water to the trees. And if you run through the woods, right when it's pouring down, you're *so* a part of it."

We see the surface of the water now. After a moment, some drops start to hit.

"I just felt a drop," said Liz, excited. "I just felt one."

Lou didn't say anything.

We see the clouds again, with the hair on the right side of the screen dancing in the wind.

After a minute or two the hair begins to get sticky from the rain.

We see the rain hitting the sea again. It rains harder now.

We keep looking at the rain-hammered surface for a while.

52.

Jim and Andy have gone back to the ocean. Jim is somewhere out in the storm, fighting the waves with his small boat. He seems lost.

53.

Andy, at a different place, speeds full of self-confidence toward the black clouds.

54.

There's a black, flashlike cut. We see Jim in the desert, walking toward the setting sun. If this were an old Western movie, he would ride on a horse. But it's not, so he's just walking. We hear a narrator's voice. This time it's not the elderly guy from the beginning. This time it's Jim's voice. He's probably looking at the scene with us.

"Rather than explaining it all now, I would prefer to say nothing at all. Have you ever sat silently on top of a big hill while the sun was slowly disappearing behind the horizon?"

The scene changes. We see Jim from far away, on top of a hill, sitting in the filtered sunlight in the grass. The grass is moving in the wind. Jim continues to narrate.

"It would be great to do it that way. I bet if we were sitting on top of a big hill while the orange sun-ball hit the ocean, molding our shadows smoothly over the hills behind, this story wouldn't need an extra explanation. We would just sit there, understanding."

The scene changes to the first one, when we saw Jim in the desert, walking toward the descending sun.

"Unfortunately, I can't bring you to the hill. I'm almost forced to explain the whole thing."

He takes another step toward the horizon.

"If you think I'm dead—in heaven, so to speak, looking back at my life—you're wrong about that. I'm more alive than I've ever been."

He lets us wait for a beat.

"Do you remember how that *senile* psychiatrist told me to write about my problems—saying that I should try to focus on the positive side while writing?

"And do you remember how my brother told me that those things that had been bugging me would be the perfect script?"

We see flashes of the movie. The first scene as Jim angrily paints the wall. Then we float over the cloudy ocean. Then we see Liz and Lou running into the waves. Then we see Jim walking along the street with Arnold. Then we see him on the train, then together with his brother, then at the psychiatrist's. Then we see Jim in the desert again.

"They made a pretty good point. They really did. It's funny, the things we need always come to us . . . and it's funny, but sometimes we just don't get it.

"The really crazy thing is that this psychiatrist—if he really was one—was right. If you start to write about yourself it's like climbing a hill. You climb a hill until you're almost able to look at yourself from a distance. And with this distance you can see things differently . . . You don't take everything so goddamn personally anymore. That's all.

"He was certainly a strange guy, though. This psychiatrist. In his crazy way, he not only told me that I should write about my problems, but he even gave me a story. I mean—do you think I was surprised when the psychiatrist told me that made-up stories usually start with a couple getting lost on an island? Of course not. I had no idea what he was talking about. It was way later that I understood he had given me the whole script in a nutshell."

The sun has almost disappeared by now. We see Jim as a small shape in front of the orange half. Some background music gets a little louder, then gets turned down, and we hear Jim's voice again.

"First, it took a lot of guts to climb this hill, but then something wonderful happened when I was close to the summit. I got a glimpse of something wonderful."

We cut to Jim on the hill again, sitting in the grass. Now the sun appears on the other side.

"All of a sudden I realized that there is some real beauty in what I've been through. I was excited about it because in this new light my life seemed kind of cool. Strange and crazy, but cool. I remember exactly when I decided to write a book about it. It was a beautiful fall day and I was riding my bicycle through the leaves. I felt so good and free, thinking about my life. I remember I shivered a little and started to whistle an old tune, just riding through the leaves."

After a rather long moment of silence, a flock of birds enters the scene, and they fly through the bright morning sun. It looks just a tiny bit too cheesy.

"Look, I'm not trying to kid anyone. I'm a writer. This story was made up.

"But the crazy thing is, it's true anyway."

At this moment the scene cuts and we are floating over the bright surface of the ocean. Smoothly flying over it. The song "Edge of the World" by Faith No More starts to play. For about a minute or two we just hear the music while looking at the water. Then the credits roll.

Daniel Wagner grew up in Moehlin, Switzerland, and is a twenty-nine-year-old builder, musician, and snowboarder. He lived in New York for part of his mid-twenties, and now he lives in Basel, Switzerland. *A movie . . . and a book* is his first novel.

A NOTE ON THE TYPE

This book was set in Minion, a typeface produced by the Adobe Corporation specifically for
the Macintosh personal computer, and released
in 1990. Designed by Robert Slimbach, Minion
combines the classic characteristics of old-style
faces with the full complement of weights required for modern typesetting.

Composed by Stratford Publishing Services,
Brattleboro, Vermont
Printed and bound by R. R. Donnelley & Sons,
Crawfordsville, Indiana
Designed by Virginia Tan